For Florence's readers, past and present, and of course for all the future ones,
and for Florence herself, who was a hero to so many —from Florence's children

For Oma —C. G.

Library of Congress Cataloging-in-Publication Data:

Heide, Florence Parry, author.
How to be a hero / by Florence Parry Heide ; illustrated by Chuck Groenink.
pages cm
Summary: Gideon is a little boy who wants to be a hero and get his picture in the paper—
but first he has to figure out just what a hero is.
ISBN 978-1-4521-2710-1
1. Heroes—Juvenile fiction. 2. Fame—Juvenile fiction.
[1. Heroes—Fiction. 2. Fame—Fiction.] I. Groenink, Chuck, illustrator. II. Title.

PZ7.H36Hr 2016
[E]—dc23

2014027996

Manufactured in China.

Design by Kristine Brogno.
Typeset in Old Time American.
The illustrations in this book were rendered in pencil and Photoshop.

10 9 8 7 6 5 4 3 2 1

Chronicle Books LLC
680 Second Street
San Francisco, California 94107

Chronicle Books—we see things differently.
Become part of our community at www.chroniclekids.com.

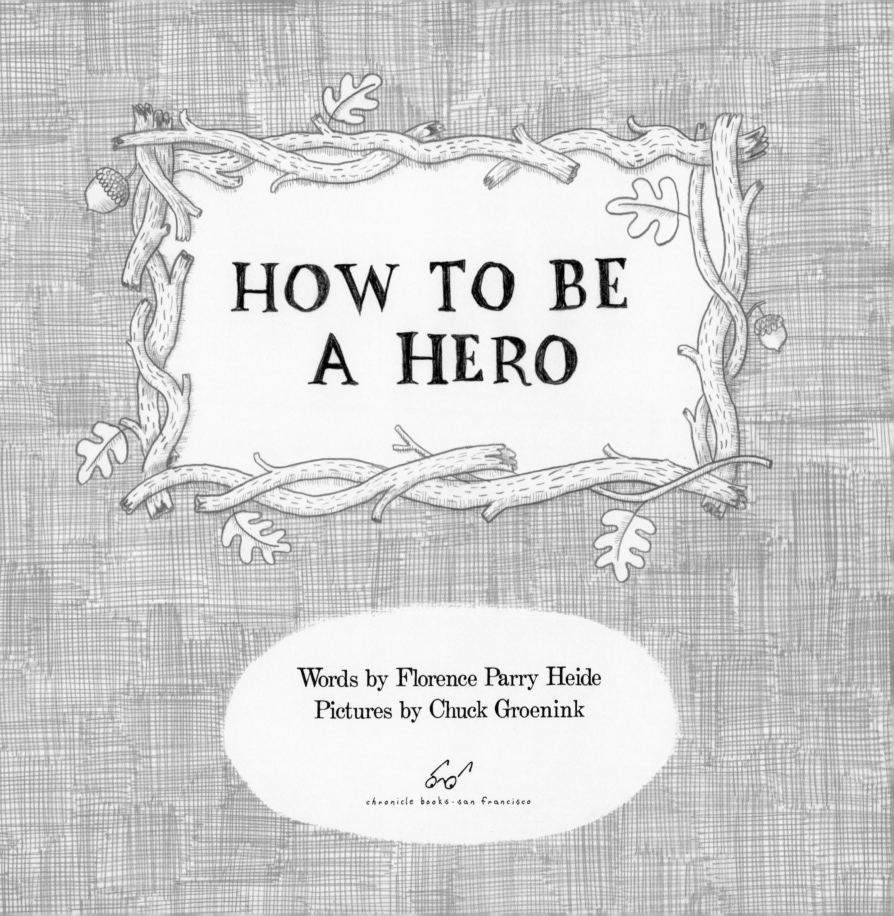

HOW TO BE A HERO

Words by Florence Parry Heide
Pictures by Chuck Groenink

chronicle books · san francisco

ONCE UPON A TIME,

there was a nice boy and his name was Gideon.

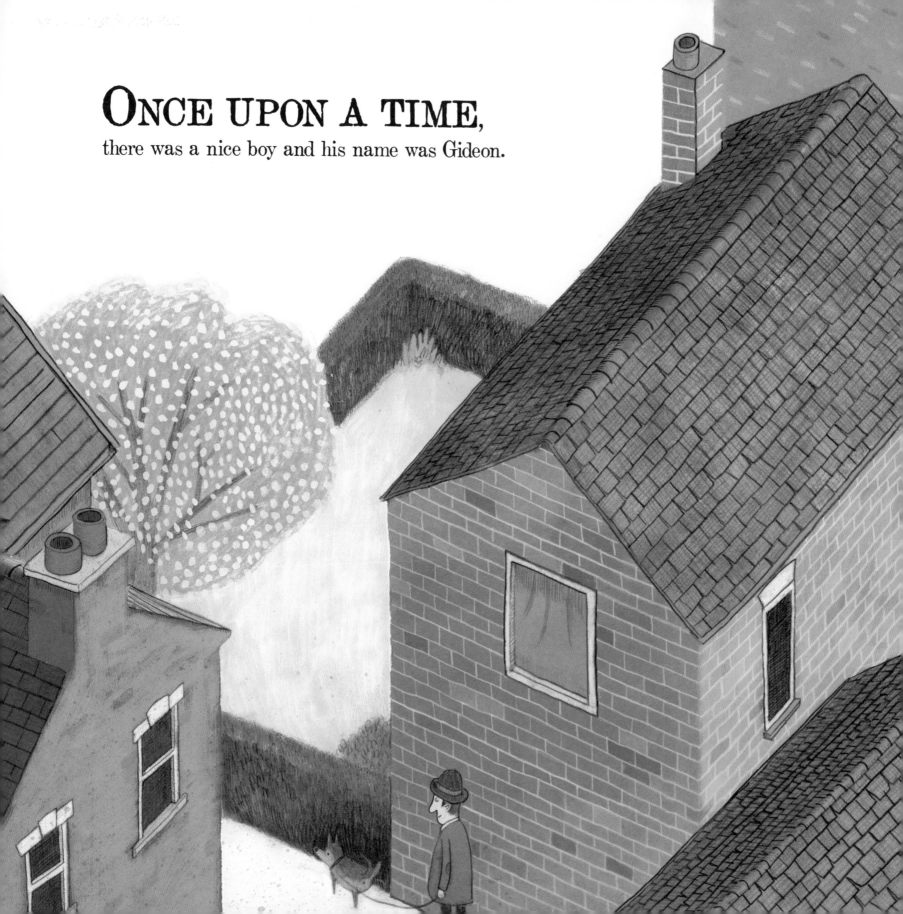

He lived in a nice house, and he had nice parents and lots of toys.

There.

That's enough for anyone.

Well, it wasn't enough for Gideon.

Gideon wasn't satisfied. He wanted to be a hero.

You know, a hero, with his name on the front page of the newspaper.

That sort of thing.

So how does anyone get to be a hero, anyway?
he wondered.

You have to be strong.
You have to be brave.
You have to be clever.

Don't you?

For instance: That one about a
princess imprisoned in a tower and
she has a weird name like Rapunella
and very long hair and this guy sees
her and says let down your hair and
she does and he climbs up her hair
and rescues her so he's a hero.

And the story where a witch gives a girl a
poisoned apple and when she takes a bite she
goes into a deep sleep which is sort of like
being dead but not really and nothing will
get her awake except a kiss and someone does
see her sleeping there and he kisses her and
he's a hero, just like that.

And Gideon thought about the one where someone has
a mean stepmother and mean stepsisters and they make
her dust and sweep and scrub so she never gets to go to
parties but a fairy godmother gives her a party dress
and glass slippers and she goes to a big party and
loses one of her glass slippers and this guy finds it
and gives it to her and that makes *him* a hero. And
just because he found that slipper.

He noticed that some of them got to be heroes just by kissing someone. Gideon didn't much like the kissing part, but he'd probably do it if he could get to be a hero that way.

Once the babysitter fell asleep watching television and he wondered
if that would count, if he kissed *her*, but he didn't think so and he
didn't do it.

One of his favorite stories was the one about this kid finding some seeds or beans or something like that and they grow up to be a great big vine and he climbs up and finds some neat things. There's a giant up there but he's asleep so the kid takes home all the good stuff, and *he's* a hero. And he doesn't have to kiss anybody.

Gideon thought about how all those guys turned out to be heroes, and he decided they hadn't really had to *do* anything or *be* anything.

They didn't have to be strong.
They didn't have to be brave.
They didn't have to be clever.

They just had to be at the right place at the right time.
That's how you get to be a hero:
you have to be at the right place at
the right time.

And you had to pay attention, you had to keep your eyes
open, or you wouldn't see someone who was sleeping or
someone with unusually long hair, or you wouldn't see
any glass slipper or any beans or seeds or anything.

So Gideon paid attention. And he kept his eyes open.

He kept his eyes open and that is how he saw the big Super Market. Seeing
the Super Market reminded him that he wanted a candy bar. His nice parents
had just given him his allowance, so he had enough money.

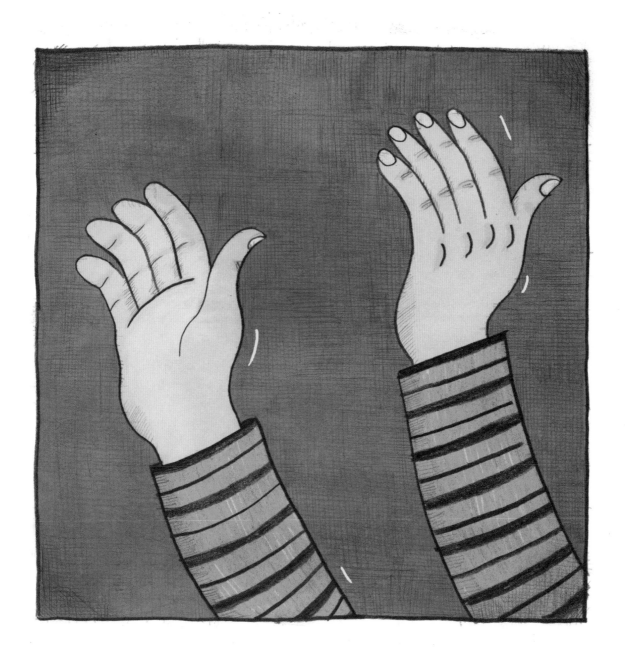

Gideon picked out his candy bar and waited patiently in line behind several other customers. He noticed there were balloons and flowers and cakes, and as he paid for his candy, people suddenly surrounded him, taking pictures, clapping him on the back, congratulating him.

Congratulating Gideon—for what? What for?

Well!

Gideon was the ten thousandth
customer to buy something
at the Super Market.

Everybody was excited. People patted
him on the back. A girl kissed him on the cheek.

(For a minute he wondered whether that might turn
him into a prince or maybe a frog, but nothing happened.)

The manager said he could come in for a candy bar
anytime he felt like having one.
His name was on the front page of the newspaper.
His *picture* was on the front page.

He was a hero.

And all because he had managed to be
at the right place
at the right time.

Good!